This edition Copyright Matthew ...
Edited by Matthew ... ...BOOKS.

All rights reserved. No part of this book may be reproduced in any form or by any means, except by inclusion of brief quotations in a review, without permission in writing from the publisher.

Each author retains copyright of their own individual story.

This book is a work of fiction. The characters and situations in this book are imaginary. No resemblance is intended between these characters and any persons, living or dead.

This book is sold subject to the condition that it shall not, by way of trade or otherwise, be lent, resold, hired out or otherwise circulated without the publisher's prior consent in any form or binding or cover other than that in which it is published and without similar condition including this condition being imposed on the subsequent purchaser.

Originally published in Great Britain in 2016 by Matthew Cash at Burdizzo Books, Walsall, UK

Ankle Biters

Matthew Cash

Burdizzo Books 2020

For Courtney and Christina,
don't stop being awesome xx

And Elizabeth Bryson
xxx

Prologue

The four sat in almost complete silence. They came to hang out at the Graveyard; their usual haunt when the weather was hot, to gossip and practice their latest renditions of boy band songs away from the tyranny of their parents.

Other than birds and wildlife the only sounds were tappings of thumbs on phone screens and the chirrups of four different types of message alert. This was a social gathering yet they spent most of the time talking to people who weren't actually there.

"Jesus man, the battery on this piece of shit goes quicker than the ones on a nun's vibrator," Courtney said as she dropped her phone onto the flat stone slab she sat on. She jumped to her feet and looked down at her friends. "Come on fucktards, let's do something."

Phones were put down, screens locked and

eyes concentrated on the girl with the long dark hair.

"What you got in mind, Corno?" Bethany said smiling up at her friend, eager to see what she had up her sleeve. The summer had been long and hot and none of them came from families that were loaded and even though they cherished the long weeks of no school, they had all started to get bored.

Courtney surveyed her surroundings, eyes searching amongst the ancient tombstones and through long yellow blades of overgrown grass for inspiration. They rested on the old stone angel that stood beneath the shade of a large tree, its wings crumbling, body wearing an ivy toga.

"Aw Hell, I don't know, but Old Flappy over there is giving me a piggyback whilst I think."

Bethany laughed and was joined by their two other friends, Meghan and Grace. Bethany was thirteen, she had longish blonde hair framing her face.

Grace was the second oldest at fifteen, blonde-haired, braces, twiggy like a model, she never said much but fit in with the others as they had known one another forever.

Meghan was the wayward one, at eighteen she had done everything before she was legally old enough. A cigarette perched on her lip, matching the one permanently tucked behind her left ear. Her crazy two-toned blue-green hair framed a heart-shaped face that was attractively chubby with its arrangement of punky facial piercings.

Courtney hopped across old stone slabs that had been poking out of the grass for decades. She hooked one long arm around the angel's neck and wrapped her legs around its body as she clung to its wings. Trickles of crumbling stone scuttled down the statue and smudged her denim three-quarter lengths. Her friends egged her on as she swiped a few buttons on her phone and posed for an obligatory selfie; tongue half out, clenched between her teeth as though she would bite it off, long white fingers flicking the peace sign and *snap*. Instant landscape portrait of a teenage girl and mournful stone face.

Courtney checked the photograph to make sure she didn't have to re-take it half a dozen times.

She sniggered loudly at the picture, "Hey looks like Old Flappy's getting off on me riding her." She stretched outwards in her friends' direction, one hand clinging to the statue's neck whilst she leant to show them the epic angel selfie.

A grate of stone on stone, the statue lurched, she lost her grip and fell into the long grass, legs in the air. The embarrassment of falling off was short-lived and she soon started cackling as her friends stood to take pictures. Courtney spread her arms and legs wide and attempted her first-ever grass-angel.

"Courtney, watch out," Bethany screamed and

grabbed her friend's arm, dragging her through the grass in time for her to be narrowly avoided by the stone angel toppling over onto the flattened grass where she previously lay.

Courtney and her friends' instinct reactions were understandably white-faced horror at her near miss, God only knew what damage the statue would've done if it had landed on her, probably crush her.

She breathed heavily and stared wide-eyed at the statue in the grass before collecting herself and flashing her trademark grin, "Holy fucking shitballs, Old Flappy tried to fucking hump me. What a goddamn lesbian."

Bethany, Grace, and Meghan sighed with relief that their friend was back to her usual loud-mouthed, dirty birdy self and joined in with her laughter.

The four girls left St Andrew's churchyard, the sun was blazing hot and Grace had mentioned her mother making lemonade.

They forgot all about one of the historical statues in the churchyard as it lay face down in the long grass, the first time it had moved since its erection over three hundred and twenty years previous.

Chapter 1

1692

The town knew about witches. The country was slowly purging itself of Satan's daughters, but some of the old hags were wilier than others.

They had always had their suspicions about Ma Lacey, her new-fangled ways in medicine were a tell-tale sign of witchcraft. They knew she was a great help to their community; she had saved a lot of lives with her preventions, lotions and potions and homemade medicines.

When the Mayor's daughter had been caught pregnant out of wedlock with that loathsome farmer's boy, she had provided the necessary means to terminate the unwanted pregnancy before any of the other townsfolk knew of the scandalous behaviour and brought shame to the Mayor's house.

Similarly, Ma Lacey had been the one to turn

to, sometimes even before the people had waited for the solitary town doctor to be sober enough to give them his attention.

But once the new man, the witchfinder, arrived in town with his band of crusaders, he instantly singled her out and no matter how many times she pleaded and protested, no matter how many little bouncy babies she had brought safely into the world, no matter how many children she had saved from potential pneumonia and worse, he ordered her to be trialled as a witch.

Once *'Witch'* was cried the townsfolk turned against her for fear that they would be taken as one of her coven. They would be spared if they gave evidence against her. Lies were spun, truths exaggerated and Ma Lacey was convicted and accused as a witch.

They burned her at the stake in the town square on a Saturday, they waited until the Witchfinder said the first stage had been completed, then they doused the embers, cut down her charcoaled skeleton, dismembered her and carried her pieces to the far corner of St Andrew's churchyard.

The witchfinder wrapped her remains in cloth soaked with holy water and had the local stonemason erect a stone angel above the spot where she was buried.

There were no words, just an unspoken rule never to remove the statue, as it protected the town from any curses Ma Lacey would have uttered as the flames licked at her calves.

Of course, even though there were no other markers, this story didn't die and soon, within a couple of generations, became part of the town's folklore.

2015

Uncle Rick wove between the tombstones, his night-vision goggles making everything green.

He adjusted a mask over his mouth and nose, he hated wearing the damn things, they were irritating and hot; but necessary. St Andrew's churchyard had suffered enough vandalism over the past week. First, the bloody kids had wrecked one of the churchyard focal points, Old' Ma Lacey's Angel, then came the bloody infestation. *Moles*.

They weren't easy to get rid of.

That's why Father Lutz had called in the best exterminator in town, the best in four counties.

Uncle Rick was known by all the townsfolk, always in his trademark army gear, he was the man to see if you needed to get shot of unwanted pests.

Uncle Rick pushed his shovel into the remaining molehill and lifted the soil away to expose the tunnel.

He pulled out a cylindrical object that looked like a white stick of dynamite. The label called it Big Destroyer. He lit the three-inch blue fuse with the lighter his Papa gave him and rolled it down into the hole. He waited long enough to see the smoke from the gas bomb plume out of the hole before filling it in so the gas could work its way through the network of tunnels.

As Uncle Rick turned to head back to his van, he heard a scrabbling behind him.

With an expression that said that he had seen it all before, Uncle Rick watched as the hole he had just dropped the bomb down rapidly begin to cave in as something attempted to escape.

"Ho, then, you cheeky little fucker, you shoulda just let that old sodium nitrate sing you to sleep." Reaching to a holster on his hip he withdrew a BB pistol. He carried it with him for the bigger rodent infestations, every so often there would be a reckless escapee and it was always fun to shoot at stuff.

Uncle Rick grinned as he saw the mole's big front diggers break through the surface and its little twitching star-shaped nose reach up for fresh air, wisps of gas coiled around it.

He waited; he was a good aim but still wanted to make sure he didn't miss.

Boy, he thought as the mole slowly extracted itself from the ground, *it's a big bastard*, no wonder they had wrecked the graveyard.

The creature sat on the mound of dirt and Uncle Rick aimed. *Give it a few breaths of fresh air. Make him think he's safe.* The rough, calloused pad of his index finger began to squeeze the trigger. Then, what appeared to be a small dark arm, shot out of the hole, grabbed the mole by the loose skin at the back of its neck and dragged its velvety ass back underground.

A squeak of pain followed and then a sickly squealing sucking noise. "What in the name of holy fuckery?" Uncle Rick switched his flashlight on and stepped towards the aperture.

He shone the beam of the flashlight into the smoking mole hole. Illuminated in its trajectory was the decapitated head of the mole that had been snatched.

Something moved just out of reach of the torch beam and dragged the mole head out of sight, protecting its food. Uncle Rick yanked the shovel out of the ground and quickly covered the entrance to the hole. Whatever the infestation was at St Andrew's cemetery was, it wasn't just moles.

Uncle Rick stormed across the graveyard, back towards the entrance to his van, he'd have to tell Lutz it was something bigger, fuck knew what though. Nearing the gravel path that ran to the main gate he never saw the fresh hole until his boot sunk into it.

He fell heavily, his leg vanishing up to the knee. When he landed his breath whooshed out of him and his knee snapped loudly, his scream filled the night. Excruciating pain shot up and down his leg and he knew he had broken it.

Why did he have to leave his goddamn phone in the van?

His wife was always moaning about him never having it in his pocket in case of emergencies.

He pushed down onto the turf with his hands and good leg and attempted to pull himself out of the hole. Something cold and slippery slithered and curled up inside his trouser leg. He imagined an octopus tentacle or snake. Whatever it was he was stuck tight and he could feel it sliding slowly upwards, the grip constricting. He had dropped the flashlight and shovel as he had fallen, but he managed to reach the shovel. He began to dig rapidly at the grass and dirt but from how low down he was and how long the shovel was, it proved to be nigh on impossible to cut through the layer of grass, let alone the soil. Uncle Rick scrabbled at the grass with the shovel and yelled as whatever had wrapped around his leg journeyed upwards towards his thigh. He was sure it was a snake.

He was getting nowhere with the shovel so threw it ahead of him and tore away chunks of grass and soil with his bare hands. The slippery cold, slithering thing pushed upwards beneath the loose-fitting leg on his boxer shorts. He felt his balls and scrotum tighten like a couple of dried walnuts as it slid around his genitals. *Oh, please God no, not there*, Uncle Rick prayed and dug more furiously, a fingernail snapped back like flaked almond. The probing moved between his thighs, along his perineum. Uncle Rick quickly yanked down his trousers and looked at the thing in his pants.

A filthy grey thing that looked like an intestine snaked across his thigh and into his shorts leaving a wet muddy trail. Rick felt it slide toward the base of his butt crack, he grabbed at it and pulled hard.

A scratching and scrabbling came from right in front of him as something dug its way out of the ground.

Just as the end of the thing found a suitable orifice Uncle Rick shrieked in pain and fear as the thing in the ground unearthed itself from the muddy hole.

They grew rapidly like seeds in a time-lapse video. Amidst wet patches deep in the ground, in the pelvic regions of corpses long turned to bone and powder. The ones born in the oldest remains had it the easiest, they didn't have to push and claw at putrid rotten flesh, they sought sustenance straight away.

Those born in bodies intact had to force their way out of loose hanging, liquefied flesh, the fresher the body the harder the work. But they were persistent and even though it took hours, days even, to break through their rancid cages and the hard-wooden prisons, they never grew tired or quit.

They knew Mother would show them the way.

They burrowed in the soil, pushing it away and tunnelling like moles. They fed on anything alive, pushing earthworms into their toothless mouths, mashing and mushing the soft bodies with their hard gums, sucking the juices and moisture greedily.

Though there was plenty of the minuscule variety of life beneath the surface they craved a more substantial feast. However, their sightless eyes needed guidance, they awaited Mother's call.

Chapter 2

Meghan saw herself on the CCTV. The footage was always behind by about five seconds. She watched herself shuffle up the aisle like a punk zombie, the case of beer was like a rock to bash someone's brains in. She threw a toothy grin at the camera and flicked her blue and green fringe off her face. Her black vest top showed way too much cleavage, which was always intentional for purchasing alcohol at the convenience store. She knew Josh would be working the evening shift.

Josh was fat, geeky, acne-splattered, twenty-two, a nerd, and deeply, head-over-heels, in love with her, and most other living things with boobs. Meghan didn't particularly like him, he stank of sweat and wanking, but she wanted booze regularly and still had another couple of years before she was legally old enough to purchase it.

"Uh oh, here comes trouble," Josh sniggered from behind the counter and threw down a paperback he had been lost in. He pushed thick-framed spectacles up a greasy nose.

Meghan grinned politely, as though it was the first time he had ever said that opener, "Hey Joshua, you're reading a book."

He nodded to the paperback and flipped it over, it was a dog-eared Stephen King novel, "You should totally check this dude out, man. King rocks."

Meghan pulled a face, "You know I'm always too busy having a good time to sit down with a book, besides all them words." She was a regular bookworm; she just didn't want to add any more to Josh's masturbatory fantasies.

"Hey, that a new nose ring?" He said instantly changing the subject, his eyes flicked quickly down to her cleavage and back up again.

"Yes, it is, thank you for noticing," again the sickly-sweet smile as she placed the crate of beer on the counter and flipped him a note.

When Josh winked at her, it was more psychotic twitch than wink, his overly large mouth went up at the corner showing his orange teeth. "Gotta keep my eye on stuff." He scanned the beer and opened the till to insert the money. A three-tone door alarm signalled the presence of another customer entering the store.

Instinctively they turned towards the sound of shuffling feet.

A filthy vagrant walked past the end of the aisle. Meghan put her hand over her mouth to stifle an outburst of laughter before picking up her beer and turning back to Josh.

"Dude, you have a great evening," she sniggered sarcastically and moved towards the store entrance. She gasped in disgust and pointed at something out of Josh's eye line, before miming sticking her finger down her throat and then leaving him to it.

Josh visibly deflated, he fucking hated the winos coming in here. He could handle the kids who wanted beer, if they were nice to him, he would usually let them buy it, just as long as the boss wasn't around, but the winos he hated. Most of them came in regularly and most tried their best to pocket something. Usually booze.

Josh flipped the counter hatch and left the checkout to investigate. When he had got to the route the vagrant had taken upon entering the store, he grimaced at the floor, "Aw man for fuck's sake."

A long trail of slush was left on the white floor tiles where the vagrant had been. Thick browns, red and yellow it looked exactly what it smelt like, blood, piss, and shit.

"What the fuck man?" Josh carefully stepped a foot either side of the trail and followed it across the shop. He followed the mess past a display of pasta sauce jars and stopped in his tracks.

"Dude, that's fucking gross."

The vagrant was wearing a camouflage jacket that was covered in dirt and God only knew what. A thick soup of red with dark red lumps coated his chin. The man squatted. Josh saw that he wasn't wearing any pants. It was clear by the state of the guy's naked legs and buttocks that the yucky stuff on the floor had come from the man's butt. Josh felt his dinner leave his mouth in a hot, thick fountain as he gazed in horror at the man's ass.

The cheeks had been torn to shreds, flaps of skin and globules of fat and muscle were on show like the damn thing had exploded. Its centre was a black bloody hole, bigger than a fist and it dripped crimson and brown.

Something flopped out of the wound and hit the floor with a wet slap. Josh retched again and groaned.

The vagrant turned lazily to face him, that was when Josh recognised him, "Uncle Rick?"

Everyone in town knew Uncle Rick, he was one of the more colourful characters. Uncle Rick's eyes fluttered open as though the lids were heavy in sleep. There was something not right with his pupils, they were dull and lifeless like they were painted on. Uncle Rick opened his mouth like he was about to say *Hi* and a mouthful of blood seeped out.

Still squatting like he was taking the most stubborn of shits, Uncle Rick reached a hand out towards Josh and grabbed a fistful of shirt.

Josh squealed and tried to pull away and did one of the most stereotypical horror movie blunders. In the one and a half seconds it took for Josh's left Nike to slip in the offal on the floor, he had already imagined the whistling sound effect that would accompany such a mishap as this. He landed hard and painfully and before he knew it he was lying on the tiles looking up at Uncle Rick's ruined asshole as he squatted over his face.

Elbows and hands slipping in shit, Josh tried to back away as something pushed its way out of the gory, cavernous hole.

Something dark-grey, which looked like a rotten human foetus pushed its ugly blind head out of Uncle Rick like a freakish prolapse, nudging aside chunks of shit and viscera with a partially formed nose. Little grey webbed hands reached out for Josh's face like a baby for its bottle as it dripped onto him. Josh opened his mouth to scream and something grey and snake-like shot out of Uncle Rick's ass and forced itself down his throat like an endoscopy tube.

Chapter 3

"Everybody's got their demons,
Even wide awake or dreaming,
I'm the one who ends up leaving,
Make it okay..."

Courtney increased the volume. *Why not?* She practically had the house to herself; her Mom's boyfriend was in the basement playing wizard-shit on his *Sexbox*, nothing could tear him away from the fugue of computer graphics and marijuana clouds.

She used her constantly bleeping phone as a microphone, today's teenager preferring it to the hairbrush and sang along to one of her favourite bands.

"See a war, I wanna fight it,
See a match, I wanna strike it,
Every fire I've ignited,
Fade into grey."

She danced around her room, the chorus blasted from the iPod speakers, the floor of her bedroom looked like an explosion in a thrift store. She had emptied her entire wardrobe trying to find an outfit to wear for the party.

Her two friends Bethany and Grace had done the usual trick of telling their parents they were staying over at Courtney's for a couple of days and that they'd be fine as there was always a responsible adult about. It wasn't a complete fabrication as Greg would be in the basement and Courtney's mother would be in and out in between working virtually non-stop at the gas station.

Meghan rarely bothered to tell her folks what she was doing unless she needed use of the car.

Courtney swiped her phone screen a few times and let out a squeal as she received a message from her friends telling her to let them in. She quickly checked in the mirror to make sure she looked cool, but also that she hadn't tried too hard to make sure she had tried too hard to look cool.

"Pffff, fuck it, it'll have to do." Which was teenager for 'I look awesome.'

She ran out of her bedroom, grabbed the stair bannister and bolted down the stairs. Making a detour to the front door, she pulled the basement door closed on her Mom's boyfriend and went to greet her friends. The three girls barged right in as soon as Courtney opened the door, Meghan came in last carrying the beer.

"Come ladies, let's get fucked up."

"What time's Christina back, doll?" Bethany asked her as she aimed herself towards a big plush settee.

Courtney's Mom was cool and her friends all loved her laid-back attitude.

"About ten probably, unless some deranged fucktard employee decides to quit again last minute." Courtney slumped down beside Bethany and cheered as Meghan put the beer on the coffee table.

"Is Gregory down in the twat cave?" Meghan asked, it was common knowledge that Courtney wasn't fond of her mother's boyfriend, but his folks let her and her Mom live there when they had no other place to go.

Courtney nodded, "Dude's gotta fucking stash of weed down there so we'll probably not even see him. Probably even takes a piss down there for all I know."

Grace sat down and smiled her big twinkly brace-filled grin and said the phrase that somebody has to say before every social gathering, especially those involving copious amounts of alcohol. To not do would surely be a bad omen, submerge the party in a swamp of bad vibes.

"Let's get this party started bitches."

Beer cans cracked, disgusted noises were made at the loathsome taste of the cheapest alcohol they could afford, music blared and fun ensued.

What was once Uncle Rick shuffled from the convenience store, combat pants and shorts crumpled at his ankles. After a few initial teething problems with walking this way, what was once Uncle Rick moved in the direction of the one who had broken the seal. Mother was growing at an excessive rate now she had fed on the young male in the store. The vessel that would carry her until she had reached full term, Uncle Rick, should suffice.

Using her umbilical, she had devoured as much of the nutritional succulents from Uncle Rick's body as her partially-formed stomach could contain. Just enough was left in the husk to perform the task necessary.

The One who awakened her wasn't far, she could sense it was a female, young and bursting with life as it should be. She would locate The One and make the call. Then her babies would come.

"And I was like 'Jeez Matty, write her a damn

book why don't you?' Woman's in love. I mean the guy's alright I guess, he has a good beard and cute kids, aside from that he looks like the offspring of a walrus and one of them ginger cows." Courtney showed the girls a photograph of her mother wearing a t-shirt with a picture of who she thought was the best writer in the world.

Grace rolled her eyes heavenward, "Thanks for the goddamn life story Corno but you were going to order the damn pizza."

Courtney gave her the middle finger and ran into the kitchen to ring the pizza parlour.

Meghan lit a cigarette and opened another can of beer. The second one always tasted better than the first. She thumbed through her Facebook newsfeed and something caught her eye amongst the torrents of bullshit statuses and endless selfies.

A photograph from one of the town's tabloids; LOCAL LEGEND HAS HISTORIANS

SPOOKED.

The picture showed the stone angel Courtney knocked over the other week, lying in the long grass in the cemetery, one of its wings snapped off completely. They were looking into getting it restored, but in the meantime, the local historians and old fuddy-duddies were pooping their panties about some old folktale that went with the statue.

Old Ma Lacey was the name beneath an ancient sketching from the town's museum.

One of the last women in the area to be tried, sentenced and executed as a witch.

She had been a local medicine woman who concocted her remedies for numerous ailments. Some great hoo-ha was implied and the town, most likely aided by the town's doctor, who had been made to look a fool on more than one occasion at the methods of Old Ma Lacey's miracle cures and she was burned at the stake.

Her remains were buried in the churchyard

beneath the old stone angel. Since the vandalism of the statue, the local clergyman had complained about a mole infestation.

Meghan grinned mischievously and tagged Courtney in the article before tuning herself into Bethany and Grace's conversation.

"Just because I don't think Freddie Schweiz is hot does not make me a fucking lesbian," Grace said astonished and took a minuscule sip from her beer. "I'd rather cut my fucking tits off with a spoon than let that retard anywhere near me."

Bethany cackled, saw that Meghan was paying attention and asked her opinion on the boy she fancied at school. "Meghan, Freddie Schweiz, yes or no?"

Meghan let out a laugh that was more like a bark, "Definitely not. One he's too young, and two, he's too skinny. Now his older brother Reggie, now I'd spin on his face all day long!"

Bethany laughed loudly and Grace blushed a little at Meghan's filthy talk.

Courtney bounced into the room like an overexcited joey kangaroo, "Pizza is on the road. What you witches cackling about?"

Bethany was about to get Courtney's opinion on her latest crush when something knocked the front door. Well, it was more like something *hit* the front door. The four girls looked at each other and at Courtney, as it was her home.

"Well, it ain't the pizza guy," she said as if that would be enough.

"So, go and see who, or *what*, it is," Bethany instructed.

Courtney seemed doubtful and a bit frightened. She hated answering the door unless she was expecting something and the way it was just a solitary knock like someone had thrown something against the door freaked her out.

She shook her head, "No way. Unless they use the doorbell or shout 'fucking pizza', I'm not answering it. Nu-uh."

Meghan stubbed her cigarette butt out on an

empty beer can and stood up muttering something about babies.

Her friends watched with slight apprehension as Meghan opened the front door, blocking their view from whatever was the otherwise of it.

They heard her gasp and then shout, "You dirty, fucking pervert!"

Courtney and Bethany ran to the door just in time to see one of Meghan's booted feet kick out at something. A whoosh was heard as the air was knocked out of somebody's lungs.

They crowded around her and stared at the half-naked guy sitting at the foot of the steps leading up to the house.

There was something wrong with him, aside from being naked from the waist down and covered in blood and mud.

A vacancy in his eyes suggested he was completely oblivious to anything around him.

"It's the tramp from the store, he must've followed me," Meghan said, happy that she had worn her Doc Martens that night.

"Mmmkay, what the hell is wrong with him?" Courtney asked peering over Meghan's left shoulder.

"He fucking reeks is what," Bethany said over Meghan's right, fingers pinching her nose.

The three girls stood at the top of the steps, looks of repulsion on their faces. The man sat with his legs splayed wide and his unnaturally swollen belly poking out and over his genitals. Even though the lighting wasn't good they could make out the dark puddle he sat in.

"Eeew, has he pissed himself?" Courtney said holding a hand over her mouth and nose.

Before anyone had a chance to answer her, the vagrant opened his mouth as though he was about to speak or vomit. His lips drew back and his mouth widened beyond its normal boundaries until they all heard the crunch of his jaw break.

An ear-piercing banshee shriek wailed from

the stretched black hole.

"Woah, fuck that shit," Meghan said and quickly slammed the door shut, bolting it behind her.

Grace appeared in front of them, wide-eyed and terrified, "Holy motherfucking shitballs, what the fuck was that?"

Meghan shrugged and tried to look cool. She was the eldest, these guys looked up to her. She had to set an example regardless of whether or not she was secretly petrified. "Just some fucking wino pervert who followed me from the store. If he doesn't fuck off we'll call the cops."

Grace went even more wide-eyed as she eyed the empties on the table. The last thing she wanted was for her folks to know about the alcohol.

"Relax, he'll not stick around now he's had a boot to the balls and besides it's freezing out there and he screams like a girl," Meghan coolly lit up another cigarette, she turned to Courtney,

"You reckon Greg will give me a joint?"

"Sure, maybe if you suck him off before my Mom gets back."

Meghan looked like she was seriously considering it, much to Courtney's disgust.

"Maybe after the pizza's got here. I wouldn't want to ruin the taste."

Their little bellies fluttered with excitement when they heard Mother's call. Now they had a purpose. They could leave the cemetery and finally seek warmth. They scrabbled with dirty little fingernails and tunnelled through the soil. Over and around water pipes, cables and long-dead cadavers alike, they crawled as fast as their tiny bodies would allow.

Soon there would be warmth. Soon there would be more substantial sustenance.

Chapter 4

The pizza guy dropped the food off thirty minutes later and even looked around outside for the weirdo wino who had seemingly scarpered. Like stereotypical teenagers they ordered way too much pizza, using every last cent of money Courtney's Mom left. The music blared across the room as the girls stuffed their faces.

Courtney heaved herself up and picked a box with two-thirds left.

"I better take this down to *Him* else my Mom will probably bitch." She nodded towards the cellar door that sat in the wall between the lounge and kitchen.

Meghan hurled a pizza crust like a boomerang at Courtney's back, it struck her on the back of the head, "Bullseye!"

"Bitch!" Courtney called out without even

turning around.

"Hey, get me a joint off Greg please." Meghan whined, "Weed goes so well with beer and pizza."

"Why, does that taste like shit too?" Grace said picking at her second slice of pizza, she wasn't a fan of the famous takeaway dish.

Courtney opened the cellar door and started down the stairs, calling as she went, "You better not be whacking off over midget porn."

Meghan turned to Bethany and Grace, "You two ever done weed before?"

Bethany and Grace exchanged glances. Bethany was ever eager to impress the older girl whereas Grace didn't give a shit, she nodded and then said like it was nothing, "Oh yeah man, all the time"

Grace chuckled incredulously at Bethany knowing full well that it was a blatant lie but chose not to say anything to embarrass her friend. Instead, she shook her head and told the truth as far as she was concerned, "I personally hate the way the stuff smells. It makes me feel sick."

Meghan rolled her eyes, "But yeah man when you take the first drag you feel yourself start to numb and drift away, you don't care about shit like that."

"Yeah," Bethany said, mimicking Meghan like she shared in her reminiscences. "Totally."

Grace was about to say something hopefully witty, but definitely sarcastic when they heard a high-pitched squeal come from the opened cellar door. Courtney came running out of the black opening, face white as bone and screamed, "Babies."

Her friends huddled around her as she shivered and shook with shock.

Meghan tried to get some more information out of her, not entirely certain that she wanted to know the answer to this mystery. When your friend's stepdad was constantly glued to his computer and someone came running away from him shouting *babies*, the only thing she could think of was child pornography. Meghan knew this was a sensitive subject but unfortunately lacked any tact.

"My fucking God is he jerking off over baby porn?"

Courtney frowned amidst her tears and garbled something incomprehensible whilst shaking her head. Meghan pushed Courtney gently towards Grace and headed to the entrance to the cellar to see for herself.

"I'm coming with you," Bethany said joining her, Meghan was glad for her company.

Leaving Courtney to be comforted by Grace, the two oldest girls started down the cellar steps. Meghan didn't understand why Greg hadn't attempted to come out and proclaim his innocence, there was no way Courtney's shriek would not have alerted him. Even if he was wearing headphones that racket would have gotten through.

The wooden steps were stereotype poorly lit cellar steps, the only source of illumination coming from a naked lightbulb and the TV blue hue from Greg's computer monitor.

What was it about people and their cellars being poorly lit? Bethany thought as she followed Meghan, her parents' place was the same. She vowed there and then that if and when she had her own digs at any point and she had a cellar, she would light that baby up like it was a fairground ride. They were about five steps from the bottom when they heard a weird, wet sucking sound.

Meghan froze for a few seconds, screamed and then spun around on the step.

"Go, go, go get out." Her face a rictus of horror as she physically spun Bethany round and shoved her hands on her back. The fact that the sight was enough to spook Meghan was enough convincing for Bethany to be equally as frightened.

They bolted up the stairs, the disgusting sound effects from the unseen image would haunt Bethany for a long time. Meghan and Bethany charged from the darkness of the cellar slamming the door behind them. Meghan leant against the door breathing hard, hands over her face as she tried to process the image.

Greg slumped in his computer chair, covered in things. Half a dozen dirty grey forms hung off him. At first, she thought they were rats or filthy rags, or she really didn't know what she thought they had been in the three-second glimpse she had gotten. That was until the thing that perched on his shoulder turned to look at her, its bulbous head and empty eye sockets honing in on her presence at the foot of the steps, its mouth a black and bloody gash, more wound than mouth. A snake-like appendage wrapped tightly around Greg's throat, squeezing open a freshly dug hole. It mewled at her, a diseased infant, and went back to sucking on the blood pumping from Greg's neck.

Courtney had been right, they were babies, but deformed, blood-sucking, demonic, fucking zombie babies.

Meghan tried to regulate her breathing; all she could do was stare at Courtney who peered out over Grace's shoulder. Their eyes said it all, they had both seen the same thing, it was no trick of the light or beer-induced hallucination.

Bethany was equally as scared as Meghan, even though she hadn't visually witnessed the scene down below, the sound had been enough. She opened her mouth to speak, not that she had any idea what she was going to say when a loud thump at the cellar door made her words turn into a scream.

Rough scrabbling scratches resonated from the cellar side of the door, Meghan instinctively jumped away and stood with her friends.

"Let's just get the fuck outta here," Grace

shouted, she was the only coherent one of the four, but the state her three friends were in was substantial evidence to suggest that she had something to fear. She hurried towards the front door, unfastened the bolts and lock as fast as her shaking hands would allow and drowned out the already raucous noise with her own petrified scream.

Standing at the foot of the porch steps was the fragrant vagrant Uncle Rick. Uncle Rick's clothes, skin, and muscles had been split down the middle from the navel upwards. A shrivelled crone stood where his skeleton should be.

Hair sparse and matted about her leathery bird-like head, her eyes sparkled with a beautiful blue luminescence, a striking contrast to her withered, disfigured figure.

Heavy bulging breasts the colour of autumn leaves drooped to her waist, the nipples elongated and dripping some rancid lactation. Thin, frail arms with long-clawed fingers reached out to the girls like a gesture for help. Uncle Rick's skinned upper torso hung behind her like the top half of some sick latex Halloween onesie, his split face and arms flapping like a hood and sleeves.

She opened her lipless mouth and spat out a thick mixture of black onto the ground, making thick liquid hacking noises. Still wearing Uncle Rick's naked lower half, the hag moved towards the first step.

Grace slammed the door shut still sobbing hysterically. All had seen that terrifying vision.

Meghan slammed the bolts across a split second before a spindly withered arm shot through the letterbox and snagged a handful of Grace's hoodie.

The cellar door splintered and the lights went out.

A lot of things happened at once, the lights died and the cellar door crashed open.

Bethany fumbled for the torch on her phone whilst wrapping her arm around Courtney's waist.

Dozens of blackened shadows the size of dachshunds came from the cellar doorway, she didn't have time to register or see them in detail before she kicked out at one. The toe of her shoe made contact with something squishy and it flew back into one of the others. She pulled Courtney in the direction of the stairs.

Grace wasn't stupid but she was scared beyond all rational thought. The hag grasped her hoodie and pawed at her to try and gain purchase on her flesh.

"Leave your fucking hoodie!" Meghan screamed at her, her fingers finding the zip in the darkness. The light from Bethany's phone ping-ponged back and forth across the wall as she and Courtney raced up the stairs. Meghan followed suit, dragging Grace with her and kicking out at anything that moved. She pushed Grace towards the stairs as something wrapped around her ankle like a rope. She didn't stop, whatever it was would be going upstairs with them. The weight of it made her leg heavy as though she wore a plaster cast. She fought her way up the stairs yelling as she felt tiny vicious arms wrap around her and begin to claw at her jeans.

With a flicker, the lights came back on as they made it upstairs.

Bethany and Courtney called out to their friends, words of frightened encouragement.

The grey-black figures of crawling zombie babies were everywhere. They climbed as quickly as their little hands and knees would allow, the same blue glow in their eyes as the hag outside. The slime and grime covering their hands enabled them to use their hands like the suction pads of chameleons, they scrabbled up the stairs and along the walls.

Courtney spotted the one clinging to Meghan's leg, its blackened gums clamping down on the heavy-duty material as its fingernails scratched and its umbilical coiled tighter, like a baby python. Being the first to witness the strange abominations swarming her home meant that she had either gotten over the shock or her sanity had well and truly fractured.

She reached forward and with Bethany's help, pulled Grace and Meghan into the nearest room and shut the door.

"Get this fucking thing off me!" Meghan yelled, shaking her leg. The zombie baby managed to make a hole in the thick material and was pushing its fingers inside to try and make it bigger.

Courtney didn't want to touch the slimy little thing but knew she had to save her friend. She pushed the toe of her shoe against its side and shoved as hard as she could, but the thing didn't budge. Her brain was reminding her what to do, she knew what to do, everyone knew what to do, *in theory*. It was a zombie and everyone knew how to destroy a zombie, the fact that it was a zombie baby shouldn't make any difference.

She searched the room for something heavy and hard. The bedroom was the guest room and it was crammed full of books, her Mom was a heavy reader, she eyed the bottom shelves where all her mother's first edition hardbacks were.

Not caring about physical or sentimental value, Courtney crouched and picked up a signed Stephen King, one-thousand-page hardback and held it above the zombaby's head. With a magical war cry, Courtney smashed the book down on the top of the baby's skull. A sickening wet crack churned her guts up and the thing made a pitiful mewling noise. A dark leaking fissure opened up, cracking its head from the soft spot down to the bridge of its nose.

She brought the book down, again and again,

sending splatter upon splatter of dark congealed blood and brain everywhere.

She dropped the book and sat on her ass in the middle of the room gagging and retching at the remains of the baby attached to Meghan's leg. The head had been destroyed, all that was left was the oozing spinal cord and grey body. She watched as the arms and legs slowly went limp and the baby unfurled from Meghan's leg.

A multitude of thuds at the bedroom door let them know they only had a few moments before the swarm would break into the room they were in. Bethany and Grace started pushing one of the heavy bookcases across the doorway but froze when they heard a massive crash from downstairs. The front door. A loud high-pitched cackle, like that of a stereotypical Halloween witch, echoed throughout. The hag was now in the house.

Meghan and Courtney both got their phone's out to call for help, upon seeing this Courtney took charge, "Call the cops, I'm calling my Mom."

Bethany and Grace barricaded the door and pushed themselves up against the bookcase hoping that the door would hold against the repetitive bangs of the babies.

Chapter 5

"The cops are on their way," Meghan shouted. She hit end on her phone.

Courtney ended her call, "So's my mother."

The bookcase trembled against the door as the zombabies increased their onslaught with more vigour. Bethany and Grace clung to one another and dug their heels into the carpet.

The cackling of the witch sounded louder, they assumed she had reached the summit of the stairs. They all heard her crackling voice as it shouted with glee, "My babies!" Lots of excited, but at the same time corrupt, baby gurgles rang out as their Mother approached. A few of the infants squealed with frustration, their hunger hadn't been sated and this was their only way of communication.

The girls heard the witch make cooing noises; a repulsive suckling noise filled their minds with visions of rotting dead babies suckling from dry, leathery milk sacks.

Meghan wasted no time since phoning the police, she opened the bedroom window and was leaning out to see if there was any way they could climb down. A sheer drop of twenty feet between the window and hard ground meant the option of jumping was as hazardous as waiting for the witch and her children to finish them off, even though it was probably an easier death.

Courtney moved to Meghan's side and was about to point out the risks of jumping when the pair of them saw dozens more black things dig their way out of the stony ground like a swarm of fat black rabbits. As soon as they had broken through the crust of the ground they crawled towards the house, umbilical cords trailing behind and between their legs like tails.

"Oh fuck there's even more of them," Courtney shouted, tears in her eyes again, she pulled the window closed when she saw the first of the new wave begin to climb the side of the house.

They needed to block the window but aside from more of her mother's vast book collection, there was nothing more they could use to help them.

In a matter of a few seconds, the first of the new wave of babies was at the window, it's toothless mouth gnashing at the glass and it's umbilical lashing back and forth like a riled snake.

Grimy grey mucus smeared across the glass as it dribbled and whined against the pane.

"We're trapped," Grace said when she saw the faces at the window. And when she said that, the witch let out a mighty cackle and a huge lightning-shaped crack split up the centre of the door.

Knowing they had found the door's weakness the babies began hurling themselves at the fissure, it would only be a matter of a few minutes before they were through.

A glimmer of hope sparked up inside them as they heard the blare of police sirens from outside and saw the red and blue lights paint colours on the ceiling.

Ignoring the gruesome babies pawing at the window, Courtney tried to spot the police cars. She was disheartened when she saw just one car. A fat bald cop got out of the passenger side and shoved his cap on, seemingly oblivious to the swarm covering the house.

A thinner cop slammed the door of the driver's side and pointed at the furrows of soil that had been unearthed by the burrowing babies. The fat cop put his hands on his hips comically and shook his head in disbelief.

Courtney scowled at Meghan, "What did you say? They've sent Laurel and motherfucking Hardy!"

Meghan's face fell, "I said we had intruders."

The fat cop nudged the thin one and pointed

at the house. They both instantly drew handguns and slowly approached the house.

Courtney couldn't bear to watch; she had seen enough horror films herself to know how this would pan out.

The cops would be that dumbfounded and sceptical to what was before their eyes that they would be overwhelmed within a matter of seconds.

The thin cop stopped in his tracks and bent down to pick something up, he quickly pulled off his jacket and Courtney realised what he was doing.

She thumped her hands against the window. "You stupid goddamn pea-brained cop."

The thin cop swaddled the baby in his jacket, the baby's black cord whipped out and latched onto his neck like a giant leech.

Courtney turned away knowing the police would be of no help. She looked mournfully at Meghan and shook her head.

The door to the bedroom splintered in and in a surprisingly premeditated gesture, the witch thrust her head through the door, paying no attention to the spikes of wood piercing her flesh. And as if she knew the girls had a tendency for favouring movies of the horror genre and had somehow foretold the works of Stanley Kubrick a few hundred years before his time, the witch grinned a black-toothed grin and said, "Heeeeeeeeeere's Mommy!"

The girls screamed in unison as the witch forced the door open an inch. The bookcase lurched, spilling books everywhere and shunting Grace and Bethany forwards.

Because the hole was big enough for the witch's head, it was just the right size for one of the babies to squish into the room.

Courtney and Meghan began hurling books at the undead baby as it plopped through the hole and onto the bookcase. Another filled the hole and started squeezing through almost instantly.

The thing on the bookcase crawled towards Bethany and Grace. Its umbilical lashed out and locked on to the top of Bethany's head. Grace threw herself across the room to where Courtney and Meghan crouched in fear.

A sharp crack came from the window behind them and they heard a multitude of gunshots come from outside. The cop had finally come to his senses.

The three girls could only stare in horror as Bethany's eyes rolled back in her head and her body danced with convulsions when the baby's umbilical delved and rooted down through her skull and into the jelly of her brain.

The bookcase was thrown to one side as the remnants of the door exploded, sending Bethany and her attacker flying out of the way.

Old Ma Lacey stood in the doorway; she had shunned Uncle Rick's skin.

In all her naked glory she was like a skeleton covered in wet autumn leaves. Wispy strands of white hair blew around her face and head like cobwebs.

She barely acknowledged the three panic-stricken girls huddled together beneath the window sill as she staggered on matchstick legs over to Bethany's body. She made a soft, gentle cooing sound and reached out. The baby which was attached to Bethany's head crawled up her outstretched arm like a monkey and perched on her shoulder, one arm hugging her neck. Old Ma Lacey crouched down towards Bethany's lifeless body, her bones and joints creaking and popping like drying wood.

She held one spindly claw behind Bethany's head and raised her in the air.

The girls could only watch as the witch lifted their dead friend's corpse over their heads and placed her black crack of a mouth over her nose and lips. A repulsive sucking noise came from the witch and the pigmentation started to run from Bethany's skin. It was obvious what the witch was doing, the more she sucked on Bethany the more her own body began to take on form. Her muscles thickened, her hair became more plentiful and her dried desiccated appearance became more succulent.

Bethany's corpse withered and shrivelled more and more with each second, the babies filled the doorway, watching their Mother with eternal love.

"Put the girl down!" Came a masculine voice from the hallway. The fat cop appeared heroically outside the bedroom door, he was shirtless apart from a filthy gunk-stained, once white vest. He looked like an overweight Bruce Willis from the *Die Hard* films, covered in sweat, a handgun in each hand. The babies from the hallway scrabbled into the room and swarmed at their mother's feet. One took too long in getting past the cop and he stomped a big foot down on it, grinding its skull into the carpet.

Old Ma Lacey shrieked like any mother would

at the heartless destruction of one of her children and flung the skeletal remains of Bethany onto Courtney, Meghan and Grace's laps, her mummified grinning skull staring up at them.

Grace shrieked and kicked Bethany's corpse off of them and buried her face in Meghan's armpit as the closest babies smothered it scavenging for forgotten morsels. Their little fingers poked and delved, eager to find something left.

Old Ma Lacey faced the fat cop and hissed like a cat, one word, "fat." The cop's eyes bulged in their sockets, he dropped the gun in his right hand and brought the fist to his chest. Ma Lacey cackled as she squeezed at the air between them like she was crushing the policeman's heart. The cop collapsed to his knees with a loud crunch as his kneecaps shattered. He fired off two quick shots of the gun before falling face down at the witch's feet. One shot took out the bedroom window showering the girls in glass and letting the babies from the outside gain entrance, the other entered Old Ma Lacey's left eyeball and blew a fist-sized exit through the back of her skull. In the split second, before brain gunk plopped down obscuring it, the girls could see straight through Ma Lacey's head.

Chapter 6

Ma lacey staggered, weak like the decrepit old hag she resembled. She turned, hunched over the girls protectively. Her eye had been obliterated by the bullet. Blood and gore ran down her face like passata.

The babies from outside slid over Meghan, Grace, and Courtney. Their mother was injured, that's all they cared about. Dozens of the rotten dead gathered at her feet, hugging at her legs for their mutual comfort.

Ma Lacey's remaining eye squinted and she bared her teeth at the young girls. She wanted their youth and vitality. She needed it for her regeneration. Her spindly hand reached towards Grace's ankle. The toughened fingers clamped around her leg and Grace's shriek brought the girls out of their frozen stupor.

Grace kicked at Ma Lacey's arm and was soon

joined by Courtney and Meghan. With a word from Ma Lacey the babies smothered and swarmed Meghan and Courtney. No sooner had one been kicked away did another take its place. Ma Lacey hauled Grace up by her ankle despite her thrashing protests. The babies coiled their umbilical cords around Meghan and Courtney's arms and legs, the vigour of which they fought against their bonds was no match for the multitude of stinking, secreting flesh that trapped them.

They could only watch helplessly as Ma Lacey prepared to do the same to Grace as she had to Bethany. *This is what's going to happen to all of us*, Courtney thought, squealing as one of the babies stuck a cold, grey tongue out to lick the tears on her cheek.

Then something weird happened.

Ma Lacey let out an animalistic roar that sounded like nothing human, she dropped the screaming Grace onto the floor and clawed at her face. A thick soupy, pinkish substance oozed from her eye hole along with wispy tendrils of white vapours. Ma Lacey collapsed to her knees as her face seemed to cave in on itself and melt. Her skin bubbled and popped like cheese on toast beneath a grill. Gloop dripped onto Grace as she scooted away.

Courtney looked at the melting witch, saw the opened cylindrical tub of table salt rammed into the back of the hag's deflating head and up at her mother Christina, who stood in the doorway.

The babies cried and wailed and covered their dying mother like ants on something sweet. The ones restraining the girls hissed aggressively at Christina as she yanked the top off another salt cellar and sprinkled it over the babies holding her daughter and Meghan.

The salt granules did not affect the babies.

Courtney looked at her Mom expectantly. She smiled awkwardly and showed her the baseball bat she had also brought. Christina swung the bat at the babies holding Courtney and Meghan. Grace cowered behind as she batted away.

The dead infants rapidly lost their viciousness now Ma Lacey was just a bubbling puddle on the floor.

Christina hauled the two girls up and Courtney jumped into her mother's arms.

"How did you know what to do?" Courtney muttered to her mother.

Christina rolled her eyes, "Duh, I'm a horror fan."

Meghan looked at Courtney, "You actually told her the truth on the phone?"

Courtney nodded and smiled.

Christina eyed the remaining zombabies as they rolled around wailing in the thick custard of their mother's remains like pigs in mud.

"Let's just get out of here before they decide to avenge her."

Christina turned to lead the girls back down through the house.

Meghan couldn't believe how calm and cool Courtney's Mom was handling things. Like she was expecting it like it was nothing unusual.

"Guys!" Grace shouted and grabbed hold of Courtney's arm. The four of them turned around and stared in open-mouthed terror at the scene in the bedroom.

The little grey-black forms of the babies were slowly melting, their grey faces sliding off their skulls, everything adding to the mess on the floor.

This should have been a good thing, the end of the monstrous zombified babies, but as they dripped and dribbled like treacle a new bigger form began to materialise on the floor. "Get to the car now," Christina screamed, shoving the girls before her.

Chapter 7

Christina ushered the girls through the house, offering words of encouragement and blatant insults.

A low rumbling came from the room above, as they ran through the lounge downstairs, the ceiling began to crack and rain down plaster dust.

"Move it you goddamn fat bitches!" Christina screamed and pushed them towards the front door.

Courtney leapt out of the front door, down the steps and straight for her Mom's car.

She yanked open the nearest door and dove inside. She scooted over to the passenger side as her Mom pulled open the driver's door. Meghan and Grace got in behind them and barely had a chance to slam the doors before Christina fired the ignition.

Christina crunched the car into reverse and drove away from the house. An explosion of timber frames and other materials came from the house as something large burst from the upstairs window taking a large portion of the wall with it.

Christina stuck the car into first and sped away.

Meghan and Grace stared at the thing that had jumped from the house. The light was poor but they made out a distinctly humanoid shape.

It moved what should be a head in the car's direction and lurched after them.

"It's following us." Grace cried; her voice riddled with despair. Christina flicked her eyes to the rear-view mirror and could see the thing staggering at quite an excessive speed behind them.

"Someone gonna tell me what the fuck is

going on?" Christina stared at her daughter accusingly as she floored the accelerator. Courtney burst into tears and muttered something indecipherable.

"It's the statue," Meghan said from the back seat.

"What fucking statue?" Christina asked in the mirror.

"Old Ma Lacey's," Meghan began.

Old Ma Lacey, Christina thought that sounded familiar but she couldn't remember why or where from. *Sounds like some wicked old cat lady*, a mangy old harridan.

That's it, Christina remembered where she had heard the name from. As a kid, her Gran used to tell her the tale of the last witch to die in Indiana. She'd tell it to her and her sister every Halloween, partly to make sure they behaved, partly to scare the living shit out of them.

Granny Lewis, her mother's mother. She would sit all hunched up beneath a green tartan blanket in a chair by the fire as Christina and her sister would sit on the rug, mouths agape at their grandmother's scary stories.

It was her first introduction to the scary story; it was no wonder she grew up into the horror freak she was.

They would sit and listen as Granny Lewis sucked her wrinkled mouth around a boiled sweet, her face crinkled but her eyes never more alive than when she was storytelling. She told them many a legend about the surrounding areas, ghost stories and the like, the happenings taking place in the locality made them even more believable and fearsome.

"Old Ma Lacey was the last woman to be killed as a witch in this state. Hundreds and hundreds of women, housewives and spinsters alike were tortured and brutally murdered for being in league with the Devil." She'd have another few sucks of her candy whilst this snippet sank in. "Of course, there were no such things as witches, these were just outcasts, oddballs or promiscuous wenches. People, *God-fearing* people, were afraid of what they didn't understand, of things that didn't seem natural to them. They still are. Some of these ladies were in tune with Nature, they knew how to make lotions and potions from the flowers, weeds, and roots at their feet."

Granny Lewis would always cackle like a Fairy-tale witch herself at this part.

"Occasionally, of course, they would find solace and comfort in dancing and cavorting in the woods. Very liberating is being naked in nature. Most people would shun these women, though some were no doubt allured by their mysterious ways. They meant no harm and would always help best they could, anyone who asked. But now and then one of their potions wouldn't sit right with someone and they'd get ill, or worse- die. That was when the witchfinders would start their accusation and these poor women would be trialled and almost certainly sentenced as a witch. They would run their ludicrous tests, the so-called witchfinders, of which almost all would fail miserably. Then they would bind them naked to a wooden stake on a big bonfire in the centre of town. Everyone, old and young, healthy and ill, would be made to watch as the Witchfinder shouted their crimes and burned the poor souls. Sure, some would cry nasty foul obscenities at the townsfolk. People they had helped and healed don't forget. And cast verbal curses over the lot of them. Wouldn't you if it were you being burnt just because people didn't like your strange ways?

"Well, the last lady in these parts was Old Ma Lacey. Old Ma Lacey got under too many people's skins, she would help where the doctors couldn't and brought many a man and child back from knocking on Death's door when the doctors had pronounced them lost. But most of all she helped girls in trouble. Girls who had fallen with child out of wedlock. Sometimes she would terminate the pregnancies safely, sometimes she would help deliver the town's babies like an old-fashioned midwife. But it was her methods and the helping of unmarried sinful women that got her accused, that and a fondness for a gentleman's touch. They caught her and bound her atop of a bonfire, all the townsfolk, many whom she had helped into the world, spitting and crying *witch, witch, witch!*"

A few more sucks of candy and a sip of a coffee laced with something special would be necessary before Granny Lewis would finish her tale. "Old Ma Lacey, oh she was different though. Even now certain folk believe she was the genuine article, a real witch. Whether she sold her soul to Satan or worshipped Mother Nature didn't make any difference.

They say when they tied her to the stake she muttered something and all the town's women clutched at their bellies as though suffering phantom pregnancy contractions.

When the witchfinder and his men lit the bonfire, the sound of a hundred babies crying echoed in the heavens and some folk say they saw wispy spectres of aborted foetuses dancing in the smoke. The fire was left burning until all that was left were blackened bones and ashes. The skeleton and ashes were loaded up onto a cart and buried in the churchyard.

The local preacher said prayers over her grave and a statue of an angel was erected on top.

"Of course, this was just a sign of respect and no doubt guilt from the townsfolk, but rumours started that it was to keep Old Ma Lacey in the ground and that it should never be removed. And rumour turned into legend as it sometimes does. But one thing I know for certain, if there was an ounce of truth in all that, I would not want to be around if they ever move that old angel to build some fancy pants apartments or such, no sir. 'cause if I were Old Ma Lacey I'd be mighty pissed off, wouldn't you?"

Christina and her sister would always giggle a bit at Granny Lewis' cuss word and she would cackle like the witches in her stories and send them off to bed with a sweet-smelling kiss on the cheek.

Christina gripped the wheel hard, her knuckles tight and white, could it be true? The crazy shit she was witnessing seemed to verify that and now with the girls mentioning the statue and how someone had knocked it over the other week, it seemed even more likely. She turned to Courtney, "It was you wasn't it? You knocked the bloody thing over."

Courtney's expression confirmed this without her even having to speak. Christina closed her eyes and swore before returning her eyes to the road.

"I didn't do it on purpose." Courtney whined, "it's been there for hundreds of years, I didn't think it would budge with my fat ass hanging off it."

Christina shook her head and sighed. It wasn't her daughter's fault, she was just being a kid and fucking around, she was a good kid, hell she was certainly a better teenager than Christina had been at her age.

"Oh my God, it's getting closer!" Grace squeaked, suddenly making everyone jump and Christina swerve the car.

The rear-view mirror showed a giant figure half-running, half-crawling behind them up the road. Christina drove towards St Andrew's churchyard as fast as the car would go. A mad cackling came from outside and lightning split the dark sky into fragments. A sudden deluge of rain fell so heavily Christina had no choice other than to slow and hit the wipers. Then the engine simply died and all the power to the car ceased. All four of them screamed as the car stalled but the three youngest looked at Christina for guidance. She tried the engine again but knew it was futile. This was the witch's doing. She knew they weren't far from the cemetery, maybe that was why they had been made to stop, maybe that was where they could be safe.

She turned to Courtney and gripped her hands tightly, "Now baby, you know I love you loads, right?"

Courtney nodded, tears streaming down her face, "I love you too, Mom."

"I want you to take Meghan and Grace to St Andrew's, try and get into the church, you'll be safe there."

Courtney shook her head but could tell by her mother's stern look it was the only hope they had.

Christina turned to the girls in the back focusing on Meghan as she was the oldest, "Run as fast as you can. Get inside the church. Stick together."

Meghan nodded and took Grace's hand.

Christina hugged her daughter, "Go."

Chapter 8

Christina watched the three girls ran, hands linked, away from her and hefted the baseball bat onto her shoulder. She flicked the lid of the trunk open but stopped when she heard heavy footfalls in the rain. She spun around and gasped at the abomination.

Standing at about fifteen feet tall was a twisted, blackened tree-like old crone.

Strands of long black hair fell over grey leathery skin like trickles of oil.

The hag was hunched up and abnormally proportioned. Christina thought she looked like a Xenomorph in a Halloween wig. In the light from the street lamps Christina could see dark-black bubbles move and boil beneath the thing's skin, they were the heads of the undead babies. Old Ma Lacey had absorbed all their energy to create this new and terrifying form. Beneath a long, dripping hooked-over nose, a dark mouth opened and she could see crooked rotten teeth. Even though she was petrified, Christina wanted to buy the girls some time. She gripped the baseball bat tight and forced a smile on her face. "Woah dude, you're so fucking awesomesauce do you know that?" She shouted excitedly, sounding like an extra to a Bill and Ted movie.

Old Ma Lacey hissed and stepped closer.

"You know everyone these days looks back upon the witch trials as something barbaric, don't you? The witchfinders, dirty little, sexually frustrated, women-hating Christian extremists?"

Old Ma Lacey stood still; a low rumbling came from her throat making her sound like an angry dog.

Christina risked a step forward. "Oh, I can tell you're angry and why the fuck shouldn't you be? They killed you because they didn't understand you, didn't agree with your radical changes, things aren't much different now. But why are you here?"

Ma Lacey spat a bucket of black onto the asphalt and pushed a wet word from her new mouth, "Vengeance."

Christina pointed the baseball bat at the witch whilst fumbling behind herself for something in the trunk. "But there is no one left alive from those times. That was three hundred years ago or more. What is the point?"

Ma Lacey's hubcap-sized eyes twinkled.

"Their blood still runs in this town, I can smell it everywhere, especially in you and she who awakened me."

"But how is killing all their ancestors going to make up for them killing you? Don't tell me you believe them all to be watching from the afterlife. My grandmother told me all about you, she said that you were at one with Nature, that your types refused to believe in all that Mumbo-jumbo. So why come back for revenge?"

Ma Lacey laughed a hideously deep monstrous

laugh, "For my own personal satisfaction."

Christina nodded mournfully, she had run out of things to say, she was surprised she had lasted this long. Holding what she had fetched from the car's trunk behind her, she swung the baseball bat round as hard as she could into one of Ma Lacey's huge kneecaps.

The bat broke in two but not before splintering Ma Lacey's kneecap and making her roar like a dinosaur in pain.

Christina turned and ran as fast as she could.

Courtney skidded around the corner, amazed to see the cemetery gates still open. A pest control van sat empty by the entrance, she hoped that meant someone else would be about.

Meghan and Grace caught up with her, their breathing rapid from exertion.

Courtney swiped her drenched hair from her face and pointed to the gates.

They ran into the churchyard, the street lights

offered little illumination after they had passed the first few gravestones but they knew where the church was. They sped across the muddy ground. Grace let out a quick yelp and they heard a sharp crack over the torrential rain. Meghan stopped when Grace fell, she'd put her foot down a rabbit hole or something, she lay on her side screaming in pain. Just from the angle she lay and the way her leg stuck in the ground Meghan could tell it was broken.

Courtney wasted no time and crouched, her mother's courage finally blossoming inside her, she hooked one of her friend's arms around her neck and tried to help lift her. Meghan copied her and ignoring Grace's protests they heaved her up off the ground. They continued their journey to the church, finding it locked with a large padlock. Courtney scanned the ground for something to break a window and spotted a shovel sticking out of the earth and left Meghan with Grace.

Courtney yanked the shovel out of the ground and snapped her head around towards the gates.

Her mother was running full pelt like a championship sprinter, her short hair plastered to her face. She yelled something Courtney couldn't hear.

Courtney saw that she was carrying something in her hand, but before she had a chance to guess what, the galloping figure of Ma Lacey came under the orange glare of the streetlights like some *witch-cum-lycanthrope*.

Christina moaned like someone who had lost all hope when she saw the heavy padlock. She took the shovel off Courtney and smashed the lock. Aside from a few sparks from metal on metal and jarring her shoulder nothing happened. "Fuck." The church windows were too high to get in even if they did break them. She turned to see where Old Ma Lacey was.

The witch-monster stopped at the entrance as though apprehensive about stepping on hallowed ground. Her elongated arms held onto the gates as she stared at them. All over her rancid skin the babyfaces mewled and cried out their mother's concern. Then she stepped through the gate and cackled loudly. She had been taunting them. Old Ma Lacey wasn't a God-fearing Devil daughter. She was something else entirely.

Christina pointed towards the overgrown part of the cemetery and the woods it led to.

It was their only hope now. To hide.

They carried Grace as best they could across the uneven ground, tripping over toppled headstones and slipping on the mud and wet grass.

Ma Lacey sloshed through the puddles like a baby Tyrannosaur. Unlike her potential victims, she could see perfectly in the dark. Her new body was powerful and strong, she kicked headstones into dust and pursued the girls easily.

They heard her gaining on them, getting closer and closer before Grace was snatched from their arms.

Courtney, Meghan and Christina stopped and turned around.

Yet again Old Ma Lacey had Grace up in the air by her ankle. The teenager shrieked and kicked out at the monster holding her.

Christina pointed to the overgrowth and woods and shouted, "Go" to her daughter and Meghan.

She held the shovel above her head, "Let her go you bitch!"

Ma Lacey laughed and held Grace above her mouth by her feet. She was nothing but finger food. Her lips drew back and her jaw began to widen unnaturally.

Christina ran at the witch but by the time she had gotten close enough to swing the shovel, Grace's feet were already vanishing.

Courtney jumped over gravestones and dodged trees as she thrust herself onwards through the sodden grass. Meghan tried her best to keep up with her as they made for the woods.

A small JCB sat by a fenced-off area and that's where Courtney went wrong. She saw the digger's scoop resting above the ground and swerved past it when suddenly the ground subsided and she fell into a sloppy muddy hole.

Old Ma Lacey batted a hand the size of a car door against Christina and swatted her out of the way like an insect. She cackled as she watched her fly across the cemetery like a ragdoll, crashing hard into a gravestone. With increased vigour from her recent snack, the witch hurtled through the cemetery towards the remaining girls.

Courtney was in a quagmire. Even though the

rain had stopped, the hole she was in was too deep and too wet to climb out of. The sides had given way to the deluge of rain, everything had turned to mud. She was filthy, she was drenched, and when she squinted up against the rain and saw Old Ma Lacey scowling down at her, she knew it was over. The old hag had killed her friends and most likely her mother, there was no way she was going out without a fight. Courtney raised her face in defiance to the witch, "Come and get me then, bitch!"

A blazing light broke the witch and the teenager's death stare and the rumbling of the bulldozer's engine was enough of a distraction.

With a war cry, Christina leapt onto the back of Old Ma Lacey and swung the shovel down on her skull.

The shovel blade sliced downwards through the witch's head, cleaving her face in two. Christina jumped from the shrieking witch as she toppled forward on top of Courtney.

Courtney flattened herself into the muddy wall as the witch fell into the hole and thrashed about in agony as she tried to yank the shovel from her head. Her mother's arms reached down for her and she somehow got out of the hole.

Courtney fell into her mother's arms and they both smiled at Meghan who sat panting in the bulldozer's seat.

Old Ma Lacey pulled at the shovel and wrenched it from her head. She bellowed demonically and tried to push herself up.

Christina picked up the can of gasoline she had taken from the car and emptied it over Old Ma Lacey's screaming split face as it tried to regenerate itself. She flicked her lighter on and without a word, without any witty one-liner, she flung it onto the witch and watched as the fuel ignited.

The noise was horrific and made them cover their ears.

Courtney nodded to Meghan who fiddled

about with the bulldozer's levers and pushed the stone angel that had been waiting to be re-erected toward the hole. Ma Lacey's writhing, burning body was crushed and pinned into the earth by the heavy statue. The three women stood and watched until the witch burned into ashes.

The dawn slowly brought light.

Christina held her daughter close and nodded towards a large mound of earth beside the pit.

"Fill it in, Meghan." They watched as Meghan went to work with the bulldozer, messily filling in the grave. The storm that had come to their town passed and as the last of the soil was emptied on top of Old Ma Lacey's reburial not one of them noticed the thin wisp of smoke that bubbled from the mud. But they all, in unison, noticed the sudden ice pick of pain inside their wombs.

The End.

Author Biography

Matthew Cash, or Matty-Bob Cash as he is known to most, was born and raised in Suffolk; which is the setting for his debut novel Pinprick. He is compiler and editor of Death by Chocolate, a chocoholic horror Anthology, Sparks, the 12Days: STOCKING FILLERS Anthology, and its subsequent yearly annuals and has numerous releases on Kindle and several collections in paperback.

In 2016 he started his own label Burdizzo Books, intending to compile and release charity anthologies a few times a year. He is currently working on numerous projects; his second novel FUR will was launched in 2018.

He has always written stories since he first learnt to write and most, although not all tend to slip into the many-layered murky depths of the Horror genre.

His influences ranged from when he first started reading to Present-day are, to name but a small select few;

Roald Dahl, James Herbert, Clive Barker, Stephen King, Stephen Laws, and more recently he enjoys Adam Nevill, F.R Tallis, Michael Bray, Gary Fry, William Meikle and Iain Rob Wright (who featured Matty-Bob in his famous A-Z of Horror title M is For Matty-Bob, plus Matthew wrote his own version of events which was included as a bonus). He is a father of two, a husband of one and a zookeeper of numerous fur babies.

You can find him here:

www.facebook.com/pinprickbymatthewcash

https://www.amazon.co.uk/-/e/B010MQTWKK

Other Releases by Matthew Cash

Novels

Virgin and The Hunter

Pinprick

FUR

Novellas

Ankle Biters

KrackerJack

Illness

Clinton Reed's FAT

Hell And Sebastian

Waiting for Godfrey

Deadbeard

The Cat Came Back

KrackerJack 2

Werwolf

Frosty

Keida-in-the-flames

Tesco a-go-go

Short Stories

Why Can't I Be You?

Slugs and Snails and Puppydog Tails

Oldtimers

Hunt The C*nt

Anthologies Compiled and Edited by Matthew Cash

Death by Chocolate

12 Days: STOCKING FILLERS

12 Days: 2016 Anthology

12 Days: 2017 [with Em Dehaney]

The Reverend Burdizzo's Hymn Book (with Em Dehaney)

Sparks [with Em Dehaney]

Anthologies Featuring Matthew Cash

Rejected for Content 3: Vicious Vengeance

JEApers Creepers

Full Moon Slaughter

Down the Rabbit Hole: Tales of Insanity

Collections

The Cash Compendium Volume 1

The Cash Compendium Continuity

Websites:

www.Facebook.com/pinprickbymatthewcash

www.burdizzobooks.com

PINPRICK
MATTHEW CASH

All villages have their secrets Brantham is no different.

Twenty years ago, after foolish risk-taking turned into tragedy Shane left the rural community under a cloud of suspicion and rumour.

Events from that night remained unexplained, memories erased, questions unanswered.

Now a notorious politician, he returns to his birthplace when the offer from a property developer is too good to decline.

With big plans to haul Brantham into the 21st century, the developers have already made a devastating impact on the once quaint village.

But then the headaches begin, followed by the nightmarish visions.

Soon Shane wishes he had never returned as Brantham reveals its ugly secret.

VIRGIN AND THE HUNTER
MATTHEW CASH

Hi, I'm God. And I have a confession to make.

I live with my two best friends and the girl of my dreams, Persephone.

When the opportunity knocks, we are usually down the pub having a few drinks, or we'll hang out in Christchurch Park until it gets dark then go home to do college stuff. Even though I struggle a bit financially life is good, carefree.

Well, they were.

Things have started going downhill recently, from the moment I started killing people.

KRACKERJACK
MATTHEW CASH

Five people wake up in a warehouse, bound to chairs.

Before each of them, tacked to the wall are their witness testimonies.

They each played a part in labelling one of Britain's most loved family entertainers a paedophile and sex offender.

Clearly, revenge is the reason they have been brought here, but the man they accused is supposed to be dead.

Opportunity knocks and Diddy Dave Diamond has one last game show to host and it's a knockout.

KRACKERJACK2
MATTHEW CASH

Ever wondered what would happen if a celebrity faked their own death and decided they had changed their minds?

Two years ago, publicly shunned comedian Diddy Dave Diamond convinced the nation that he was dead only to return from beyond the grave to seek retribution on those who ruined his career and tainted his legacy.

Innocent or not only one person survived Diddy Dave Diamond's last ever game show, but the forfeit prize was imprisonment for similar alleged crimes.

Prison is not kind to inmates with those type of convictions and as the sole survivor finds out, but there's a sudden glimmer of hope.

Someone has surfaced in the public eye claiming to be the dead comedian.

FUR
MATTHEW CASH

The old aged pensioners of Boxford are very set in their ways, loyal to each other and their daily routines. With families and loved ones either moved on to pastures new or maybe even the next life, these folks can get dependant on one another.

But what happens when the natural ailments of old age begin to take their toll?

What if they were given the opportunity to heal and overcome the things that make everyday life less tolerable?

What if they were given this ability without their consent?

When a group of local thugs attack the village's wealthy Victor Krauss, they unwittingly create a maelstrom of events that not only could destroy their home but everyone in and around it.

Are the old folk the cause or the cure of the horrors?

ALSO
FROM
BURDIZZO BOOKS

THE CHILDREN AT THE BOTTOM OF THE GARDDEN
JONATHAN BUTCHER

At the edge of the coastal city of Seadon there stands a dilapidated farmhouse, and at the back of the farmhouse there is a crowd of rotten trees, where something titters and calls.

The Gardden.

Its playful voice promises games, magic, wonders, lies – and roaring torrents of blood.

It speaks not just to its eccentric keeper, Thomas, but also to the outcasts and deviants from Seadon's criminal underworld.

At first they are too distracted by their own tangled mistakes and violent lives to notice, but one by one they'll come: a restless Goth, a cheating waster, a sullen concubine, a perverted drug baron, and a murderous sociopath.

Haunted by shadowed things with coal-black eyes, something malicious and ancient will lure them ever closer. And on a summer's day not long from now, they'll gather beneath the leaves in a place where nightmares become flesh, secrets rise up from the dark, and a voice coaxes them to play and stay, yes yes yes, forever.

Printed in Great Britain
by Amazon